WONDERCOLTS FOREVER

THE DIARY OF CELESTIA AND LUNA

Cover design by Liz Casal.
Cover illustration by Laura Thomas.

Little, Brown and Company
Hachette Book Group
1290 Avenue of the Americas, New York, NY 10104
Visit us at lb-kids.com
MLPEG.com

First Edition: January 2017

Little, Brown and Company is a division of Hachette Book Group, Inc.
The Little, Brown name and logo are trademarks of Hachette Book Group, Inc.

The publisher is not responsible for websites (or their content) that are not owned by the publisher.

Library of Congress Control Number 2016932978

ISBNs: 978-0-316-26732-8 (hardcover), 978-0-316-26730-4 (ebook)

Printed in the United States of America
WOR
10 9 8 7 6 5 4 3 2 1

This book was edited by Mary-Kate Gaudet and designed by Carla Alpert. The production was supervised by Rebecca Westall, and the production editor was Lindsay Walter-Greaney. The text was set in Amadeo and Segoe Script.

WONDERCOLTS FOREVER

THE DIARY OF CELESTIA AND LUNA

BY SADIE CHESTERFIELD

LITTLE, BROWN AND COMPANY
New York Boston

Dear Diary,

Okay. It's been a **long time** since Luna and I kept a diary together (When I was in fifth grade? Maybe sixth?), but this seemed like a good time to start. This year is a **big year for both of us**. This is my last year at Canterlot High, and Luna's very first year. She's a freshman now. It will be the only time we're in high school together, and the very last year we'll live in the same house before I go to college. We're sisters, and we have our differences and fights sometimes, but I'm going to miss her.

(Did you read that, Luna?
I'm going to miss you—seriously.)

Maybe this diary will be a way for us to keep all the memories we'll make this year.

It felt so good to walk through the halls of Canterlot High again, and see all my friends after summer vacation. Some girls were away at camp, and others went on

vacation with
their families.
I only got
to see a handful
of my friends who stayed in town. Windy
Winters is a senior with long red hair and
freckles. She's the captain of the soccer team,
and the head of the Leadership Committee.
She's been one of my best friends since
sophomore year. There are woods behind the
campus, and tables out back where you can
sit and read in the sun. We spend most of
our lunches out there, talking and trying to
catch up on the homework that's due the
next period, or wondering who's going to ask
who to the fall or spring dance. It turns
out Luna is in Windy's study hall period,

CANTERLOT
HIGH

so today Windy introduced Luna to a few freshman and sophomore girls she thought Luna might want to be friends with. They were mainly little sisters of some girls we know, but it was nice to know Windy was looking out for my sister. She's great like that.

I guess that's all for now. But really ... Canterlot High is even better this year than it was last. There's something really special about being a senior and ruling the school. It's just us. No one to look up to or worry if they think you're cool. We're the ones people talk about in the bathrooms or when they walk down the hall. I can't wait to make this last year **really count**.

Love,
Celestia

Hello, Diary!

Celestia started this journal weeks ago. I know I should've written to you sooner, but I got caught up with all the things that were happening at school. **It feels like so much time has passed since I started at Canterlot High**, but it's really only been a month. Celestia has always been on so many teams and in so many clubs. She's on Canterlot High's debate team and in the archery club; she's helping with the school's fund-raiser this spring, and she plays soccer after school every day with her friends. What's CHS like for me? I haven't jumped in to a ton of activities or clubs, but I'm slowly getting the hang of it here.

I guess I can be just a tiny bit more **introverted** than Celestia. My old guidance counselor taught me that word, and it just means that it's not as easy for me to be talkative or outgoing, at least not at first. I don't know if it's something about being Celestia's little sister or what, but the first week I was so nervous at Canterlot High. Even though everyone was being really nice, I kept worrying that I'd say or do the wrong thing. I let Celestia do a lot of the talking for me. I really, really missed my friends from middle school. We all went to different high schools. Some of us went to CHS, but others

went to Crystal Prep, the private school in the middle of the city. There are also a lot of kids I haven't met before. They're from all the different middle schools in town.

This past week, things have gotten much better. I've made friends with two really smart, fun girls in my grade—Seasons and Galaxy. They're also really nice. They're both really excited about the school plays here, and they're trying to get me to audition this year for <u>A Light in Time</u>, this musical about fairies who set out to save a cursed prince. I think I might! Being on stage might be the perfect way to learn to be outgoing. **It also sounds <u>really</u> fun.**

That is the latest here, Diary. Stay tuned for more stories!

Luna ·

Dear Diary,

These first weeks of school have been **awesome**. I've been spending every second with Windy and the rest of our friends, and I think I've even gotten better at soccer (they always go easy on me when we play together—I've been to some of their games, and they're pretending to be a lot worse than they actually are so it's still fun for me).

The debate team has kicked in to full gear. We're preparing for our first competitions in December. Lately we've been debating things about Canterlot High, like the pros and cons of serving healthier, more expensive food in the cafeteria. We talked about how we can best support the girls' sports teams, and the best ways to involve the school in the community. It was during the end of one of our debate practices that it happened...

Windy was sitting outside the classroom where the debate team practices, waiting for me so we could walk home after school. I didn't realize she was listening to our debate about school lunches, but I guess she was. "You've got so many great ideas about Canterlot High," she said as we walked back.

"How have you never thought of running for school president? It just seems so obvious!" I almost spit soda all over her. I've been at Canterlot High for over three years, and I am really involved with a lot of clubs and teams, but I can't imagine being the school president. Our school president last year was Cherry Blooms, but she'd graduated. Still... she was the most popular girl in school! How could I win the election this year? I have a lot of friends, but I'm definitely not someone everyone knows.

But then Windy told me how Joyful on the Leadership Committee mentioned my name in a meeting the other day, when they were talking about who could replace Cherry Blooms. They were <u>really impressed</u> by me, and thought I'd be perfect. The elections are starting next week so they are putting a list of nominees together. Windy didn't promise anything, but it seemed like my name might be on it.

I don't know what to think! I'd never considered running, but maybe I should....

Love,
Celestia

Hi, Diary—

Principal Potts held an assembly today to talk to us about the school elections. I was sitting in the back with the other freshmen, but I could see Celestia up in the front row with her friends. Last night she'd mentioned running for school president to me, and I told her I'd help any way I could. Celestia is so smart and kind, and has such great ideas. I know I haven't been at Canterlot High long, but I can't imagine someone being a better leader than her.

Anyway—back to the assembly. Principal Potts talked about how the elections would be run, and how the Leadership Committee would submit their nominations tomorrow, and then the nominees would have to accept. She said that choosing a school president is always important, but this year it's even more important than in the past. This year

is the **First Annual Friendship Games** with Crystal Prep. Principal Potts and Crystal Prep's principal, Principal Cinch, have decided it would be a way to **unite** the two schools.

I've been to Crystal Prep once before, last fall. It's toward the center of the city. So many of us in town went to middle school together, and then came the time to choose which high school we'd attend. I'd toured both Crystal Prep and Canterlot High, but I always kind of knew I'd go to CHS, mainly because this was where Celestia went and it would be weird to go to a different school from my sister. But my best friend from middle school, Night Sky, had decided to go to Crystal Prep. So did a few of our other friends. Once everyone decided, about a fourth of our class went to the private school. We'd spent this past summer hanging out at one another's houses or in the park, but since school started I haven't heard from them as much. We're all so busy making new friends...It's sometimes hard to remember how good our old ones were.

I miss Night Sky. We used to laugh so hard together over the littlest things. She loved baking, and her mom would help us make cookies and cupcakes and then decorate them with sparkly sprinkles. We used to sit in her tree house and listen to music for hours. There were a lot of great things about today, but the idea of getting to see Night Sky more often, and to meet all her new Crystal Prep friends? That's really cool. These new Friendship Games can't come fast enough....

Luna

Dear Diary,

Today everything changed. It's weird when you can feel that happening, when life gets better in just one moment. I was in physics class when a girl I'd never seen before knocked on the door. She was holding a blue envelope. Everyone else in the class started clapping and cheering and yelling. They were so loud Ms. Thunderstruck had to tell them to be quiet so the girl could talk. Apparently, everyone except me knew what that envelope was. So I was surprised when the girl called out my name. "Celestia?" she asked, scanning the room. "This is for you."

"I knew it was true!" a boy in the back of the room yelled. Some people were clapping. I opened the envelope, and inside was a blue card that said:

WONDER Colts

You have been nominated for school president.

Please let us know if you will accept this nomination by 3 PM today. Best, the Leadership Committee.

I couldn't stop smiling. I knew Windy had said I should run, and they were impressed by me, but she'd never promised me the nomination. I almost sprinted out the room and down the hall, chasing after the girl. Ms. Thunderstruck waved for me to go. I caught up with her by the cafeteria. "Yes!" I said. "I'll accept the nomination! I'd love to run for president!"

I didn't even think about who I'd be running against, and I still don't know. I guess I'll find out at some point. But for now, I'm just excited.

And (if I'm being **completely** honest) a little nervous.

Celestia

Dear Diary,

It's so late here, and I just tiptoed through the house. Luna is in bed already, and I don't want to wake her. I still can't sleep, though....

I know it's been a while since I wrote, but my stomach is tied up in knots. I'm so nervous for tomorrow—it's the last day of the election. And I've been running against Hurricane, another senior.

Yes, **that Hurricane**. The captain of the football team and the most popular senior guy. He's tall and handsome, and always makes the funniest jokes. Every guy wants to be him, and every girl has a big crush on him. Even I think he's nice, and I'm running against him. It's not going to be easy to win, and now I'm worried it was silly for me to ever think I could. Is it really possible that people would vote for me instead of Hurricane?

Luna keeps telling me that I did everything I could. She's been such a great sister, really. She helped plan a Meet the Candidate event on the front of the school lawn, where she gave out cupcakes and cookies we had baked. Everyone drank fizzy drinks, and I told them my plans for the school. She helped me make buttons and posters. She came up with this slogan:

CELESTIA FOR PRESIDENT
IT'S WRITTEN IN THE STARS

It makes it sound like it was meant to be or something. Then tonight, she helped me with my big speech. I feel bad....I kind of snapped at her a few times when she was listening to me practice. She kept interrupting me and asking questions, or having me to read a line over again. It was driving me **crazy**! I hope she knows I'm just nervous. So nervous. I have to give the speech tomorrow before everyone votes.

I have to listen to Luna. I did everything I could. **We** did everything **we** could.

I just hope that's enough.

Celestia

Diary!

I have **SO** much news!

Today was the day of the election. After a whole month of running for president, the students of Canterlot High were finally able to vote. Hurricane or Celestia: Who would they pick as their new school president? What would they decide?

Before I tell you what happened, I have to tell you about Celestia's speech. I knew it was going to be good when she first read it to me last night, but I didn't know how good. (I got a little distracted by all the attitude she was throwing my way. Yeesh.) She stood on the stage in front of the entire school, and started talking about how many good memories she has of Canterlot High. She talked about her four years here, and everything she'd learned. She said she **really loved the school** and wanted

to be president so she could give back.
Everyone could see how genuine she was.
As I looked around, kids were nodding and
smiling while she described her ideas for
the Friendship Games, for bringing the
students of <u>Crystal Prep and CHS together</u>,
and for <u>CHS in general</u>. When she was
done, everyone stood up and clapped!! **A
standing ovation! It was crazy!!**

Hurricane's speech was fine. (Maybe I'm
biased. So what?!) He said some stuff about
the Canterlot sports teams, and yelled, **"Go
Wondercolts!"** at the end. But it didn't
have the same kind of heart Celestia's did. I
don't know; he's really popular and all, but
I don't get what everyone sees in him. He
didn't even talk about Crystal Prep or the
Friendship Games or any of the friends he
had to say good-bye to when he came to CHS.

I guess you know what I'm going to say next...Celestia won the election. **My sister, Celestia, is now the school president of Canterlot High! I couldn't be prouder!** I've even joined her planning committee, to help with the Friendship Games. I just called Night Sky and she said she's on the planning committee at her school, too. In just a few weeks, we'll be reunited again.

YAY!
Luna

I can't believe it!!!

Hooray!!

This is the best day ever!
I'm literally jumping up and
down as I write this!!
I can barely stand still!

Hooray!!

This is _amazing_!!

Dear Diary,

Okay...I've calmed down a bit. Luna and
I had three whole days of celebrating. We
went out for ice cream at the best ice-cream
shop downtown, and Windy and our friends
threw me a little party after school. It seems
like everywhere I go now, people are staring
at me. Yesterday, I was walking down the

hall when I heard two girls whispering behind me, "That's her! That's Celestia!"

As excited as I was about being Canterlot High's new president, today was a strange day. Very strange. Principal Potts called a meeting with Crystal Prep's principal, Principal Cinch, and Crystal Prep's student body president. We were supposed to discuss the Friendship Games with them. It turns out the CP president is my old friend from middle school, Crescent Moon. I recognized her immediately and went to give her a hug, but she was kind of weird. She acted like a stranger. I wondered if she didn't remember me that well, or maybe was worried about seeming too friendly in front of Principal Cinch. I've thought about her a thousand times since middle school ended, and I've wondered for so long what she was like now. But it seemed like she hadn't thought about me at all. Not even once.

Principal Cinch is a stern-looking woman with pale-turquoise skin and **purple hair**. She must be new at Crystal Prep, because she seems really young. She looks like she's barely older than me! Her dress shirt was buttoned all the way up, and

she has a plump mole on her left cheek. Her
voice is practically three octaves lower than
Principal Potts's and her face is twisted, like
she just kissed a lemon. Principal Potts
started the meeting by saying how excited
we were to build a friendship with Crystal
Prep, and reunite our students with all
the friends they'd said good-bye to years
before. She talked about how everyone in
our school was excited to see their friends
from middle school, and how we'd hoped
that by having the Games year after year,
the students from our schools would keep
in better touch. Didn't Principal Cinch
agree that this would be a wonderful way
to build a community between the two
schools? To maintain all the friendships

that so many kids lost when they went to high school?

"Yes," Principal Cinch said. "It should be fun."

She said "It should be fun" in a way that made it sound like we'd asked her to **sort through a dumpster with us**. I wondered if it was maybe just how she spoke or if the words had just come out wrong. She didn't seem to register our surprised faces.

Crescent Moon just sat there, nodding. She didn't smile the entire time. I know Principal Potts didn't want the Friendship Games to be about winning. We'd barely picked our team yet, and we hadn't even thought about training them, so I can't imagine that Principal Cinch thought we

were being competitive. After the meeting, Principal Potts told me that Principal Cinch has always been a bit odd. They haven't known each other very long, but things have changed since Principal Cinch started at Crystal Prep. The students have become much more serious, and Principal Potts wonders if maybe Cinch just has a very "_intense_" personality.

Celestia

Hi, Diary...

It's been a **weird** day. Everything started out fine, like normal. School was good. They served my favorite lunch in the cafeteria today—grilled cheese with tomato slices. I sat with some of my new friends and we talked about how funny Barley, the kid who did the morning announcements, was. Celestia and I even had a meeting for the Friendship Games planning committee, and we started talking about our team and what outfits we'd make for the big event. I volunteered to go into the city after school and look for different fabrics.

I took the bus downtown, and walked around some fabric stores. I found this **really cool** blue-and-gold fabric that we might be able to use. I took a few samples to show the planning committee. Then, right before I got back on the bus, I had this idea. Maybe Night Sky and some of our old friends would want to meet me downtown for ice cream. Crystal Prep was so close, not even a five-minute walk away. I hadn't seen them in weeks, and we'd already chatted about the Friendship Games and how cool it would be to have that day every year to catch up. I turned down the block toward Crystal Prep. I remembered Night Sky mentioning this one street where her friends hung out after school. There were tons of shops and an ice-cream place and a movie theater. I wondered if maybe I'd run into them—school had only let out an hour ago.

I hadn't even been walking a minute when I saw her. She was standing outside a clothing store with some girls I didn't recognize. They were all talking and laughing so much they didn't even notice me there. There was no way I couldn't notice her though. Night Sky always stood out to me in a crowd because of her sparkly dark-blue hair, and her pale skin shimmered in the bright sun.

I waved at her. She looked up quickly, then looked away.

"Let's go inside," she said to one of her new friends. "I want to try on that skirt...."

I watched as they all filed into the store. I know there are a hundred reasons to explain

why Night Sky did that. Maybe she really didn't see me, and I just imagined she did. Maybe she saw me but didn't recognize me. Or (this reason I don't like as much) maybe she saw me but thought it would be weird to introduce me to her new friends. I really don't know.

Whatever the reason, I've felt sad all afternoon. And Celestia won't stop talking about the fabric for the uniforms and how great the Friendship Games will be. I can't tell her that one of my oldest friends just ignored me. And that the Friendship Games don't feel that exciting anymore, not if I don't have Night Sky to share them with.

Luna ·

Dear Diary,

   Things are getting off to an okay start
with the Friendship Games. Luna found
this great blue-and-gold fabric from a store
downtown, and Windy's mom helped us sew
a few basic pieces on a sewing machine. We
made a sample skirt and shorts and even
a headpiece the girl team members could
wear. We were so busy working it took us a
moment to notice Principal Potts standing
by the door.

She stopped by the art room where we were sewing to tell us a little bit about the rules of the Friendship Games. She and Principal Cinch had decided that the teams for the games would be picked from a list of volunteers from all four grades. Each principal would consider the student's involvement on their school's sports teams, as well as the different ways the student had shown school spirit. Students on both teams wouldn't know the events they were competing in until the very first minutes of the Friendship Games. They wouldn't even see the playing field beforehand. That way they'd have to train in many different areas, promoting sportsmanship and athletic excellence. The three main events could be anything from archery to a relay race to an obstacle course. The team that won two out of three of the main events would be the winner of the Friendship Games.

We spent the rest of the afternoon making a banner to welcome Crystal Prep students to our school and wondering what those three events might be. There had to be at least one relay race or obstacle course. And I wondered if there'd be archery, too. Once the team is finalized, Windy plans on going to Crystal Prep with our team. She wants to bring over some cupcakes to try to sweeten up Principal Cinch. I wished her luck. No matter how tasty those treats are, it's going to take a lot to put a smile on Cinch's face.

Celestia

Dear Diary,

I thought yesterday was a **huge success**. Principal Potts gave us the roster of athletes for the Friendship Games. Hurricane will be competing on the team, as well as a few other kids I've known for the last four years. Windy was chosen to be on the team because of her skills as a soccer player, and I was chosen to be the team's coach. I spent the afternoon over at Windy's house, baking cupcakes and cookies, then decorating them with the blue and purple Shadowbolt colors. Then the team and I headed downtown to Crystal Prep.

When we got there, we waited outside Principal Cinch's office for a while. They were holding their own meeting about the

Games. I couldn't hear much from where we were sitting, but Cinch kept repeating the word **competition**. After a while, they let us in, and Windy made this whole speech about how good it would be to reunite with all our old friends. Even Crescent Moon seemed touched—she **actually smiled** at me. "What a nice gesture," Principal Cinch said, staring down at the purple-and-blue cupcakes. "I can tell you all value friendship very much." I'm so proud.

Then we went around the room, introducing ourselves to one another. Crescent Moon told me it was good to see me after all these years. A few of the other team members recognized old friends who had gone to Crystal Prep. We talked about how the **Canterlot Gazette** would announce the Friendship Games the next morning, and how exciting it would be to be on their front page. The team really did seem happy to see us — they even seemed nice.

At least that's what I thought.

This morning, Luna and I got up, and our parents were reading the **Canterlot Gazette**:

Crystal Prep and Canterlot High Announce First-Ever Friendship Games.

It had a huge story about the Games, and it even mentioned the names of all the different team members, including me. We talked about how exciting it was the whole way to school. But then, as we turned the

43

corner, we were **horrified**. Our Wondercolt statue, which has sat outside the school since it first opened, was painted bright purple. Purple and blue streamers hung down from every tree.

Hundreds of Canterlot High students stood on the lawn, staring up at the Wondercolt. Everyone was furious. "Crystal Prep did this," one girl said. "They ruined our Wondercolt." I couldn't bring myself to argue. There were blue and purple streamers everywhere. If the Crystal Prep students didn't do it...then just who did?

Celestia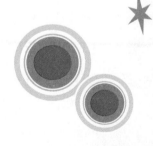

Diary!!!

I can't believe them! **This is horrible.**
As soon as I saw what they did to the
Wondercolt—our Wondercolt—I wanted to
march over to Crystal Prep and tell them they
didn't know anything about friendship or
kindness or generosity. I wanted to tell them
they were mean to come to our school and do
that to our statue, especially after how nice
Celestia and the team were to them. I mean,
come on!

Celestia baked them cupcakes!!!

But Principal Potts stood on the lawn
outside school, telling everyone to be calm.
She said she was going to call Principal Cinch
herself and tell her what the Crystal Prep
students did. But as soon as she went inside,
all the kids exploded.

"We can't let Crystal Prep get away with this!" one girl yelled.

"They're making fun of us! They think our school is a joke!" a boy cried out. As upset as Celestia was, she stepped forward. She waved her hands in the air, trying to quiet everyone down so she could talk.

"We shouldn't jump to conclusions," she said. "We don't know for sure that the Crystal Prep students did this. Let's just wait and see what Principal Potts says."

People didn't like that. A few girls started yelling that it so obviously was Crystal Prep who did this. They were sending us a message. One girl even said she wasn't being a good school president. Hurricane was probably the most upset out of everyone. "They think they're better than us," he yelled. "We have to show them we're tougher than they are!" Celestia just repeated what she said about not knowing anything for sure, and I could tell she was trying to stay positive. The crowd went back inside, leaving me and Celestia staring up at the purple statue.

I hope Principal Potts will be able to fix this. Because right now, it feels pretty hopeless.

Luna

Dear Diary,

I think my hands are **permanently purple**. I washed them over and over tonight, but I can't seem to get the purple stain off my fingers. It's hard to forget about what happened to the Wondercolt statue when I'm reminded every single time I look at my hands.

Luna and I spent all afternoon cleaning the statue outside school. The paint the Crystal Prep kids used was really hard to get off, so we had to scrub down the marble for hours. The Wondercolt is still a little weird-looking. The white marble is kind of pinkish purple now. Leo, one of the janitors, told us it might fade with sunshine and rain.

Hopefully, the marble will be shiny and white again in a few weeks. ~~Hopefully~~ ...

After we cleaned the statue, we went to watch the Friendship Games team train. They were running laps around the track. A few of them were practicing archery on the field. They all seemed really happy to be training, working hard toward our goal, and eager to forget about what happened to the statue, at least for a little while. I'm trying to keep that attitude, too, but it's hard. Principal Potts said Principal Cinch denied that Crystal Prep students had painted our statue or that any of her students would ever be involved in something so **"unsportsmanlike."** She even suggested that a Canterlot High student might have done it to frame the Shadowbolts. That sounds a bit far-fetched to me. But I have to admit, a small part of me really wants to believe that they had nothing to do with

this, and that they're just as innocent as Cinch says they are. We've already worked so hard, making uniforms and training for the Games. The <u>Canterlot Gazette</u> has already announced and set the date for it. It's already a news story. If we canceled it now, it would be such a waste of all that hard work. And even worse, everyone in town would start talking about how our schools couldn't get along.

If I'm being realistic, though, it does seem like Principal Cinch is just making excuses for her students, which only makes it harder to forgive them. Every time I look at our beloved statue I get annoyed all over again....

Celestia

Hi, Diary,

I feel like the whole school is in a bit of a funk. Ever since the statue was painted by the Crystal Prep kids, everyone has been worried about the Friendship Games. Some CHS kids don't think there's any point in having them anymore, and others think that maybe the Crystal Prep kids were just trying to be funny. Others are determined to get back at Crystal Prep with an even bigger prank. Just today, I heard Hurricane, the senior who ran against Celestia, talking to a whole group of kids in the courtyard. He was really riling them up.

"We <u>can't</u> let Crystal Prep get away with this," he said, pointing to the statue. It still isn't white yet, but it is at least a faded purply pink. "They came to our school and ruined our Wondercolt. And their principal still says they had nothing to do with it. She's even claiming a Canterlot High student might have done it. Do you believe that? Someone needs to do something about this right now!"

He didn't say what someone should do, but everyone in the crowd was talking about playing another prank—**something bigger.** They wanted to show Crystal Prep they can't mess with Canterlot High. It was almost like Principal Potts heard everything Hurricane said. She came on the speaker to tell everyone how proud of us she was. "You've kept your cool in a very frustrating situation," she said. "Remember to keep the spirit of friendship alive during this difficult time. Canterlot High will rise above!" Hearing that made me feel a little better. I noticed a lot of the kids didn't look as mad as before, either. Some even smiled when they heard Principal Potts's words.

I called Night Sky after school and
we talked for a while, and she said how
everyone at her school was really upset, too.
She said she didn't know anything about
what happened to the Wondercolt, and I
want to believe her. Then I asked her about
what happened outside the store that
day, and she said she was sorry. She did
see me standing there, but ever since the
Friendship Games were announced, all her
Crystal Prep friends have been being really
competitive and say Crystal Prep has to do
everything they can to win. She felt like
she couldn't say hi to me, a Canterlot High
student, in front of them.

That really hurt. I hate that going to
different schools has already come between
us so much. But I'm trying to focus on the
positive, like Celestia does. I have to believe

that CHS will rise above. Next month, at the Friendship Games, we will have our big moment!

Luna

Dear Diary,

When we left school yesterday everything seemed fine, but we came in this morning to chaos. We hadn't even been in class for fifteen minutes when we were called in to an emergency assembly.

Principal Potts stood onstage. Her cheeks were bright pink, and she kept glaring at the audience, like she was really mad. "There are people in this room who know why this assembly was called," she said. She looked around, but no one said a word. "Late last night, someone went to Crystal Prep to get revenge. They threw blue and gold streamers over every tree. They painted a Wondercolt horseshoe in the Crystal Prep courtyard. And, worst of all, they stole the Shadowbolt.

That crystal statue is Crystal Prep's most prized possession."

Everyone looked around, wondering if someone would stand up and admit to it. But no one did. The whole room was buzzing. Someone said Hurricane's name, and I spotted him in the fourth row with some friends. He looked just as confused as everyone else, though.

Principal Potts went on, telling us that whoever took the statue had until the end of the day to return it to Crystal Prep. "If it is not returned in the next few hours," she said, "the Friendship Games will be canceled. Please see me right away if you know anything about this." A few people gasped. A girl in my science class yelled that it wasn't fair. But Principal Potts just left the stage without saying anything else.

Windy was sitting right next to me, and she must have seen the tears in my eyes. Canceling the Friendship Games? What would happen to all our hard work? What would we do with the uniforms that we'd made, and what about all those hours the team had spent training? And I didn't even <u>want to think</u> about the headline in the <u>Canterlot Gazette</u>....

"Don't worry," Windy said. "It'll be okay."

It's fourth period now, and I'm still so upset. I keep repeating Windy's words to try and make myself feel better. I **<u>really hope</u>** she's right.

Celestia

Dear Diary,

It's me again. I can't stop looking at the clock. I'm writing this entry in Ms. Thunderstruck's science class. It's almost the end of the school day, and as far as I know, no one has come forward and said they were the one who took the Shadowbolt. I'm hoping that they will, that maybe they are just waiting until the last minute. If the Friendship Games are canceled...

...I don't even want to think about it.

Celestia

Hi, Diary,

It's been two days since the Friendship Games were canceled. No one has said anything about the crystal Shadowbolt. Celestia and I have launched our own unofficial investigation, talking to as many people as we can, asking them where they were and had they heard anything. But no one seems to know a thing. It's like it just— **POOF!—disappeared. Gone forever.** I keep waiting for someone to say they have it, but no one has even admitted to being near Crystal Prep that night.

I feel **so sad** for Celestia. She's been acting really upbeat about the whole thing. I see her in the halls sometimes, trying to smile and stay positive when kids ask her about it. But I know how upset she is. Just this afternoon, we went downtown to return the rest of the fabric we'd bought for our

Friendship Games uniforms. When we were walking out of the store, she turned to me. "The hardest part," she said, "is now things between our schools are worse than they've ever been. Crystal Prep students are really angry with us, and I understand why."

We walked up the street, passing Crystal Prep on our way to the bus stop. Blue and gold streamers were still hanging some of the trees. Principal Potts has told us there will be a cleanup day soon, when a bunch of Canterlot High students will go to Crystal Prep to take down the streamers. I hope that makes things better, at least a little bit. If only for Celestia's sake. I'm still mad about the Wondercolt, though. Why are we the bad guys when Crystal Prep has been so mean? Doesn't anyone remember that **they started** this prank war?

Luna .

Dear Diary,

Today we went over to Crystal Prep to clean up the blue and gold streamers, and scrub the yellow paint off their courtyard. A few Crystal Prep kids sat on the stairs watching us. They were all scowling, like we'd done something horrible. **It's _so_ upsetting!** It wasn't us! It was a few CHS students who wanted to get back at them, and we had nothing to do with it. I only wish we could prove that.

I ended up giving a speech today as we cleaned up. Over thirty students from Canterlot High came to help out. I told them that we hoped the Crystal Prep students would see that we wished them well. We wanted to make this better, and

we wanted them to know this wasn't the spirit of Canterlot High. As we picked the streamers from the trees, I told Crescent Moon that we were working on finding the crystal Shadowbolt. I'd make it my mission to get it back to them. I won't stop until I figure out who did this. That's the only way to make things right between our schools.

Celestia

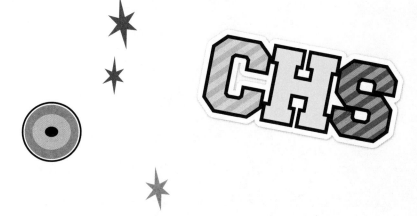

Dear Diary,
No no no no...

Just when I thought things couldn't get any worse, Luna and I came down for breakfast this morning and saw the <u>Canterlot Gazette</u> on the kitchen table. Our dad was flipping through it, and we spotted the story on the second page. The headline read:

President of Canterlot High School:

Prank Went Too Far.

The story was about how we went over to Crystal Prep the other day to clean up. But they made it sound like Canterlot High students were criminals. The **whole** first part of the story was about how much damage we'd caused. They kept talking about the crystal Shadowbolt and how no one had admitted to stealing it. Then they quoted me, but the words they put down **weren't the words I'd said**. It wasn't the <u>same</u> speech. They made it sound like I thought Canterlot High was filled with liars and thieves.

Dad said we should call up the newspaper and tell them they had gotten the story all wrong. I'm worried, though, that it wasn't a mistake. The whole time we were at Crystal Prep, Principal Cinch was watching us from her office window. She kept glaring at us, a huge frown on her face. Is it possible she told the <u>Canterlot Gazette</u> just her version of the story? How did they know we were at Crystal Prep that day? And why was the whole story so one-sided?

Celestia

Hi, Diary,

This weekend I tried to be the best little sister a girl could want. Celestia has been really down since that story came out in the _Canterlot Gazette_, so I planned a whole day in the park for us and her friends. I invited Windy Winters and some of the kids that had been on the Friendship Games team. We had a big picnic by the lake, with sandwiches and cookies and cupcakes.

Everything was **perfect**. The sun was shining. There wasn't a cloud in the sky. Everyone was laughing and having fun, and the girls were kicking around a soccer ball. It took me a while to notice the women next to us. They had a big blanket spread out under a tree. Their little girls were playing with some toys. At first I didn't understand what they were saying, but then we all heard them mention something about "Canterlot High."

"I'd never send my kids there," one woman said. "Those students are running around at night, stealing things! It's terrible!" Another mom said that Crystal Prep was just a much better school. Even if the tuition was high, it was worth it. The third woman called Canterlot High students **"troublemakers."**

We just sat there, listening to them. I was going to march over there and say something, but what? How could I argue with them? Even the biggest newspaper in town was saying that Canterlot High was filled with "<u>problem children</u>." Instead, I looked to Celestia. We'd talked to as many people as we could those first days after the Shadowbolt was stolen, but we must've missed something. Someone at CHS knows what had happened. We have to dig deeper. "We need to get to the bottom of who took the Shadowbolt," I said, and she nodded. As soon as we got home **we went to <u>work</u>**.

Luna.

Dear Diary,

This is the first day in a **long time** that I've felt better about things. Luna and I are working to figure out who took the crystal Shadowbolt. If we can find and return it, we're hoping that we can save Canterlot High's reputation. We'll prove to everyone that this was the work of just one or a few Canterlot High kids—not all of us. We still have a chance to make everything right between our schools.

We had to really think about who the thief could be. Hurricane was the one who talked the most about getting back at Crystal Prep for the prank they'd played on us. But he looked as confused as everyone else the day Principal Potts announced what had happened. Was he just pretending he didn't know about the missing Shadowbolt?

Or was it possible he really had nothing to
do with it being stolen? Luna and I wanted
to find out.

Today, after school, Hurricane and a
bunch of his friends were sitting on the
lawn by our Wondercolt (she's still a little
pink). Luna and I asked him if he knew
anything about the missing Shadowbolt
statue. "You think <u>I</u> stole it?!" he asked.

"You did tell everyone we needed to get
revenge on Crystal Prep," I said. He thought
about that for a minute. Then he told us
he could prove he wasn't the one who stole
the Shadowbolt—he shares a room with his
little brother and never left that night. We
followed him to the science wing of school,
where his little brother was doing extra
credit for his biology class.

Ocean Wave, Hurricane's brother, said he knew Hurricane didn't take the statue because Hurricane was sleeping above him all night. He always wakes up when Hurricane comes down from the top bunk, and that night he didn't. They both were so serious—we want to believe them. But if Hurricane didn't steal the crystal Shadowbolt...who did?

I wonder if maybe it was someone who wanted to impress Hurricane. He's one of the most popular kids in school. Did someone do it just to show off? Luna thinks it could be someone on the Friendship Games team. I told her I couldn't imagine one of the athletes stealing the Shadowbolt, but she said we should look at everyone very closely.

I really hope it isn't anyone we know....

Celestia

Dear Diary,

   Playing detective has been **really fun!**
We heard Hurricane and his brother's
story yesterday about the night the crystal
Shadowbolt was taken. They seemed like they
were telling the truth, but today I wanted to be
sure. While Celestia was at her meeting for the
Leadership Committee, I followed Hurricane
around for a while to see if I noticed anything
that seemed odd.

   At first I don't think he even realized I was
there. When he was walking down the halls, I'd
follow behind him. When he turned around,
I'd run and hide behind the water fountain
or in a doorway. All afternoon, he didn't do
anything that seemed weird. I even overheard
him telling his friends about what happened
yesterday. "Do you believe that? They thought
I stole the Shadowbolt!" he said. He was talking
about me and Celestia. "I had to prove to them

that I didn't. I don't like Crystal Prep, but I'm not a thief!"

I followed him for a little while after that, but it seemed useless. From what I can tell he's definitely not the one who took the statue. Celestia doesn't think it was anyone on the Friendship Games team, but then who was it?

Luna·

PS: Toward the end of the day, Hurricane caught me following him around the track. He asked me what I was doing and I just ran away. He must think I have a crush on him now. **Ugh!**

Dear Diary,

I've been so busy trying to figure out who took the Shadowbolt, I haven't been doing as much as I can as president. Today I had a meeting with Principal Potts and the Leadership Committee to talk about different events that are coming up. We're going to have a big party to help raise money for the library. The librarians want to buy new books and even put in a reading area with couches and chairs for students to relax after school. We're hoping that the whole town comes to the party to support us. There will be raffles and a DJ, and tons of food and drinks. It should be a fun night.

Principal Potts didn't mention Crystal Prep until the very end of the meeting. She said she still hoped someone would return the Shadowbolt. Maybe things would get better after that. I told her Luna and I had been trying to figure out who took it and that seemed to cheer her up a bit. We'll keep looking, but until we find it, I have a big party to plan.

Celestia

Dear Diary,

There's been so much good news lately, it's easy to forget about everything that happened in the last month. The plans for the fund-raiser are moving along. Instead of a DJ, a group of Canterlot High students volunteered their band. They all have electric-blue hair, and they sing rock songs. Luna and I just went to listen to them tonight, and they were so fun. We danced in the front row, throwing our arms up and singing along with the choruses.

Windy and a dozen of our friends agreed to bake everything for the party. We're going to have every <u>type</u> of sweet you could imagine—brownies, cupcakes, cakes, cookies, fondue. Windy said she knows how to make "rock candy," which is just sugar that looks like giant crystals on a stick. We're going to sell each one for a dollar.

Everyone is getting excited about the new library. Just this afternoon I heard some kids talking about it at their lockers. They thought it would be cool to have a place to go after school and just hang out. I'm hoping the fund-raiser will be a way for everyone to come together and move forward after the cancellation of the Friendship Games. Luna is not so sure, though. She wants to come with me tomorrow to meet the Friendship Games team at the gym. They're giving back all their equipment from the Games.

I know she thinks they might have taken the Shadowbolt, but I just can't imagine that. Would someone from my team really do something like that?

I guess we'll see....

Celestia

Hi, Diary—

So today was a **big day**. Celestia and I waited by the gym for the Friendship Games team. At about four o'clock, they all came walking up to the shed out back, carrying the last of their equipment. Lavender, a girl with bright-purple hair, returned a bow and a quiver of arrows. Autumn Frost gave back some weights he'd been using. Everyone was happy to see Celestia and chat about the fund-raiser that was coming up. The whole time I was looking for clues. Could anyone on the team have taken the Shadowbolt statue? Had we been silly for not talking to them sooner? Anyone could be a suspect.

Celestia worried they'd be upset that I thought it might be them, and the night before we got into a big fight about it. She had told me a thousand times not to ask too many questions or make it seem like we thought they were thieves. "Nobody on my team would do something like that," she cried. "Stop accusing my friends, Luna!"

But we had to talk to everyone and rule out the team as the ones who took the statue. Celestia made a face when I brought up what happened at Crystal Prep. I asked if they had any ideas about who might have taken the Shadowbolt. "It's the worst," Autumn Frost said. "And now everyone thinks we're the bad guys! They started the prank war!" Lavender didn't know anything about where the statue was, but she seemed just as upset about Canterlot High's new reputation. As Celestia and I closed up the shed and went home, I thought a lot about their answers. It seemed like they were being honest with us. But if Hurricane didn't take it, and neither did the Friendship Games team, then who did?

Luna. 🌙

Diary!

I have big news!

Something **HUGE** happened today!

For the last week Celestia and I have been really stumped. We haven't given up looking for the Shadowbolt, but we've come pretty close. Then, just last period, I was in the bathroom during study hall. I'd just closed the stall door when two girls walked in. They must not have noticed me in there, because they started chatting about Hurricane.

"He's so cute!" one of the girls said. "I stood behind him in line at the vending machine yesterday. I swear he smiled at me!" They were older than me—probably juniors. I could tell by the way they talked. Then the other girl said excitedly, "He'd be so impressed if he knew." She was about to say more, but her friend said, **"Shhhhh!"**

really loudly. She told her not to talk about it at school. She said it was "too risky."

Then the girls washed their hands and left. I stayed in the stall until I was sure they were gone. Now there's only one problem... I didn't get a good look at them. I tried to see through the crack in the stall door, but I couldn't really. I did get a great look at their shoes, though. One girl had on a pair of pink high-tops. The other girl was wearing black flats with a shiny buckle on the toe.

It's not a lot to go on, but it's something. I'm just happy we have our **first <u>real</u> clue**!!!

Detective Luna

Dear Diary,

<u>I'm dizzy!</u> All day today, wherever I went, I kept staring down at everyone's shoes. As people passed me in the hall I kept my eyes on the floor, looking for a pair of pink high-tops and the pair of black shoes with shiny buckles. I was walking with Windy after third period and she looked at me like I had three heads. "What are you doing?!" she asked. I finally told her Luna's story about the two girls in the bathroom. Then she spent the rest of the day the same as me, just staring at the floor.

Neither of us had any luck. After school, I went to Principal Potts's office to talk to her about the fund-raiser. She had the <u>**strangest**</u> look on her face when I walked in. Her eyebrows were pinched together and her cheeks were bright red. I looked down and saw she was reading the <u>Canterlot Gazette</u>. "Another story!" she said, holding up the newspaper. The headline was

Crystal Prep's Principal Reports

Applications Are On the Rise.

I started reading the story. Principal Cinch was saying how they'd gotten twice as many applications for Crystal Prep as they had the year before. She said it was because of what happened with the Friendship Games. Parents were scared to send their kids to Canterlot High now. They thought they'd do bad things, like steal or

play pranks on people. I read and reread
the story. It didn't even mention that we
had come over to clean up the streamers! It
never said that Crystal Prep had played a
prank on us first!

Principal Potts and I were so upset by
the story we barely talked about the fund-
raiser. We just sat there for a while. Then
I made a plan: We'd throw the best party
we could next weekend. We'd show everyone
what Canterlot High students were really
about. And **hopefully**, in the meantime,
we'd find the Shadowbolt....

Celestia

Hi, Diary,

Last night, Celestia and I were up late talking. I'm upset by what everyone is saying about Canterlot High, but not **nearly** as upset as Celestia is. She explained it to me while we were lying in our beds in the dark. It's her last year at Canterlot High. In less than six months she'll graduate and then go to college. She hates thinking that people in town have the wrong idea about CHS. They don't know how kind and welcoming the students are. How inspiring the teachers have been for her. "I want to be able to say how proud I am that I went to Canterlot High," she said.

It makes me really sad to think about going to school and not having Celestia there. I'm going to miss sitting with her at lunch, and planning bake sales and parties with her. I'm going to miss hanging out with her and her friends after school, the way they play soccer on the lawn by the Wondercolt statue. I've only been at CHS a short time, but we already have so many happy memories here. I hope when she looks back on her senior year she thinks of the good times, too, not just what happened with Crystal Prep.

Luna.

Dear Diary,

Everything was **perfect** for the fund-
raiser today. Luna and I worked all morning
setting up tables and chairs on the lawn in
front of Canterlot High. The band got there
early and was practicing. We kept dancing
and singing along as we hung up lights and
streamers. Windy and our friends brought
hundreds of cookies and cakes. Principal
Potts was in charge of the ring toss, and
Ms. Thunderstruck ran the basketball hoops.
All the money we raised from the tickets,
the games, and treats would go to the library.
At about noon, people started arriving.

It wasn't obvious at first. There were
so many people I knew that Luna and I

were busy greeting everyone and chatting about the new library. But after about an hour, I noticed something strange. We'd put posters up all around town and had even put an invitation in the Canterlot Gazette. But there were only CHS students and parents at the party. No one else from the town had come to support our school.

I told Luna what was happening and she looked around, a shocked expression on her face. "You're right...." she said. The whole day we waited, but no one from town came to CHS. When the party was over we'd only made a couple hundred dollars. It wasn't half of what we need to get all the books the librarians wanted.

Luna tried to cheer me up, but I feel miserable. Will Canterlot High always be known as a "bad" school? When will people forget about what happened? Are we doomed to be forever in the shadow of that missing Shadowbolt?

Celestia

Dear Diary,

You're not going to believe this. I was in Principal Potts's office during study hall today. We were talking about the fund-raiser this weekend, and how we could get the library the money it needs. Then a tiny freshman boy with green hair and glasses knocked on the door. I'd never seen him before, and it seemed like Principal Potts hadn't, either. He asked to talk to the principal alone.

About five minutes into the meeting, Principal Potts called me back into her office. She told the freshman boy to tell me what he told her. "It happened a few days after the Shadowbolt went missing. I was walking home through the woods and saw two girls hiding something in the dirt. When they saw me looking at them, they told me I better not say anything or I'd be sorry. It was kind of scary. They seemed really serious."

A lot of kids hang out in the woods behind school. Some eat lunch under the trees, and others walk through it on their way home every day. I asked him what they looked like, so I could be sure I was searching for the right girls. He didn't have the best memory. At first he said they had pink hair, then he said one had gold hair and the other had rainbow streaks in her hair. Then he said he couldn't remember, really. He also couldn't remember where exactly they were burying the statue, which was even more upsetting. The woods are so big, it could take us weeks to find it if we don't know where it was hidden.

"I'm sorry," he said. "I should've said something sooner but I was scared, and then when I saw what happened with the fund-raiser...how no one showed up...I just started here this year and I don't want to make enemies, though. I want people to like me. You won't tell them I was the one who told, will you?"

I told him we wouldn't. I was <u>**thrilled**</u>, even if he couldn't remember all the details. For the first time, it seemed like we had real information about what had happened to the statue. Maybe it was the same two girls who Luna had overheard that day in the bathroom. Maybe the Shadowbolt is hidden in the woods somewhere. If it is, we'll find it.

Celestia

Diary!

<u>I was right!</u> Those two girls I overheard in the bathroom were the ones who took the Shadowbolt. They have to be. I'm pretty sure I know why they did it: They wanted Hurricane to think they were cool. That's why they kept talking about how cute he was and how impressed he'd be if he knew.

Celestia and I searched the woods after school with the Friendship Games team. We worked with Windy, Hurricane, and our friends to cover as much area as we could, but without knowing where exactly the girls had hidden the statue, it was impossible to find. We could've had a hundred kids searching and it wouldn't have helped. That's when I came up with an idea....

"What if we give the girls a reason to come back for the statue?" I asked. "They were trying to get rid of it, but what if they needed it again? What if they had to come back and find it?"

Celestia wasn't quite sure what I meant. News spreads fast around school, especially gossip. "What if we started a rumor that the reason the crystal Shadowbolt was so special to Principal Cinch was because it had a very valuable gemstone hidden inside it?"

Celestia looked at me like I was crazy, but then Windy smiled. "Yeah—a gem worth thousands of dollars!" She laughed. Celestia understood then, and said it might just be our only chance. We'd tell a few people tomorrow, and they'd tell a few people, and hopefully the whole school would know by the end of the week. Then all we'd have to do is wait for the girls to come back to find their treasure....

Luna .

Dear Diary,

It's only been two days since we spread the rumor about a ruby inside the crystal Shadowbolt. But it seems like everyone is talking about it now. "No wonder Principal Cinch is so angry," I heard a boy in my math class say. "We robbed her!"

Today at lunch, Luna and I continued our stakeout. We were sitting at the tables behind Canterlot High. Luna kept looking over my shoulder at the woods. We ate our sandwiches in silence, waiting to see if anything odd happened. Then, just as lunch was almost over, Luna froze. Her blue-green eyes got **really big**. She suddenly stopped eating her sandwich and nodded to the woods behind me.

Two junior girls were right on the edge of the forest. One wore high-top sneakers and the other wore black dress shoes with shiny buckles. They whispered to each other, then looked around to see if anyone was watching them.

Of course **we** were watching them. But Luna quickly grabbed her sandwich and pretended to eat. I started talking loudly about the lacrosse game the night before. I didn't stop until I was sure the girls had disappeared into the woods. Then, without saying a word, Luna and I got up and followed them.

We stayed far back as they went off the trail. Then they put their hands in the dirt, brushing back the leaves and soil near a rock. I guess Luna couldn't stand watching them anymore, because she yelled out, **_"Wait! Stop!"_** The girls spun around, their faces pale. They stood up straight, like it was totally normal to be digging a hole in the middle of the woods.

"We know you're the ones who took the Shadowbolt," I said. "It's important that we get it back." The girl with the pink high-tops froze. Before I could say anything else

she turned and took off through the woods.
Her friend ran after her. Luna and I had
no choice but to chase them. We jumped
over rocks and fallen logs, and ducked under
low tree branches. We kept running until we
were almost out of breath.

The woods ended. The girls ran out into
the neighborhood behind Canterlot High. But
then the girl in the dress shoes slipped and
fell. That was the only thing that made her
friend stop running. The girl in the sneakers
turned around to help her.

Ahhhh—Luna is right next to me now.
She thinks it's **VERY** unfair that I get to
tell the whole story, Diary. I'm going to let
her finish....

Celestia

Hi, Diary—

First: a big thank-you to Celestia, my generous older sister, for letting me tell the most important part of this story. So, where were we?

That's right, the girl in the dress shoes had just slipped and fallen on the grass. Which I wouldn't wish on anyone, but it did help us catch them. They looked embarrassed when they finally got up and brushed the dirt off their clothes. "We're sorry," the girl in the high-tops said. "It's just that—we can't give the Shadowbolt back. We're sorry, but we can't." I asked them to start from the beginning. Had they been the ones at Crystal Prep that night? Did they do it for the reasons I thought they did?

"We wanted Hurricane to think we were cool," the girl with the dress shoes said. She had poufy green hair. We found out her name was Milestone, and both she and her friend were juniors. "He kept talking about how someone needed to get back at Crystal Prep for what they did to the Wondercolt. We've both had a crush on him ever since fifth grade, so we thought if we stole the Shadowbolt he would like us. Or notice us, at least." Her friend, a redheaded girl named Willow, frowned.

"We went to Crystal Prep that night and threw streamers in all the trees," Willow told us. "We painted a big yellow horseshoe on their courtyard. Then we broke in the front door and stole the Shadowbolt from its pedestal in the main hall. It was heavy, though, and it took more effort to carry it than we thought it would."

She went on with the story, telling us how they were trying to carry it down the street when they dropped it. It smashed into two pieces. They knew they were in trouble then. They'd only meant to take it for a few days, to teach Crystal Prep a lesson for playing a prank on our school. They always meant to return it. But now that it was broken in to bits, they couldn't.

They buried the pieces in the woods behind Canterlot High. They hoped at some point people would just forget about it. But when they heard about the ruby that was inside it...they wanted to check to see if the rumors were true.

I still remember Celestia's face when the girls told us the Shadowbolt was broken. I've never seen her so sad. It was like all the hope she had for finding it was gone. Sure, we knew where it was, but what did it matter when we couldn't give it back? Wasn't it worse that two Canterlot High students had not only stolen it, but broken it, too?

The girls took us to the place where they'd hid it. We dug up the pieces and carried them to Principal Potts's office. Even though Willow and Milestone seemed very sorry, Celestia told them that they had to tell Principal Potts what had happened. As we walked them all the way to the principal's office, they had tears in their eyes.

I do feel bad for them. They knew they made a mistake, and they had no idea how to fix it. They seemed so worried about getting in trouble. I guess it's too late for that now, though....

Luna

Dear Diary,

It was so hard to tell Principal Potts what had happened. I wasn't even the one who took the Shadowbolt, and I was nearly in tears when we walked into her office. She had wanted to find it as badly as I had. And now there was no hope of giving it back.

Willow and Milestone sat down on the chairs in front of her desk. They slowly told the story, and Milestone started crying when they got to the part where they dropped the statue and broke it. After watching the whole thing, Luna and I agreed—Principal Potts is the kindest, fairest principal we could ever imagine. She made sure the girls knew they had done something wrong, but she was also really kind to them. She gave them hugs when they cried. She said she understood that they were sorry. She told them they'd have to say sorry to Principal Cinch and all the students at Crystal Prep. They'd also have to do a week of detention after school.

Milestone and Willow are supposed to go

to Crystal Prep on Friday, two days from now. They're going to tell Principal Cinch what happened, and give back the pieces of the broken Shadowbolt to her. My stomach hurts, **I'm so nervous** about it. I just wish there was some way for things to be different. As soon as Principal Cinch knows the statue is broken, there's going to be

another story in the _Canterlot Gazette_ about
how bad we Canterlot High students are. I
can almost picture the headlines:

Canterlot High Students Destroy Crystal Shadowbolt

Canterlot High Students Admit to Robbing Crystal Prep

Everything is going to go from bad
to worse.

I've spent so much time wishing we'd
find the Shadowbolt. Now that we have,
Canterlot High may be in more trouble than
before. I just wish there was something I
could do....

Celestia

Hi, Diary—

Principal Potts made the announcement about the Shadowbolt statue this morning. She didn't tell Canterlot High who had taken it, just that it had been found and was being returned to Crystal Prep. She also didn't say that it was broken. I guess she didn't want to upset people any more than she had to. The sad thing is, kids were talking all day about what would happen now that the statue was found. Did that mean the Friendship Games were back on? Would Crystal Prep finally stop spreading lies about our school? I didn't have the heart to say that nothing would change. If anything, now that Principal Cinch knew the girls had broken the statue, things would probably get worse.

After school we met Principal Potts, and then we all drove over to Crystal Prep.

It was me, Celestia, Willow, and Milestone.
Principal Potts wanted us there so that
Celestia could say sorry as the president of
Canterlot High. She thought that maybe,
just maybe, it would help Principal Cinch
and Crescent Moon understand that this was
all a huge mistake.

No one talked on the drive over to Crystal
Prep. When we finally got there, we sat down
in Principal Cinch's office. Celestia held a
duffel bag in her lap. The two pieces of the
Shadowbolt were hidden inside. We didn't
want to just show up and surprise them with
the broken statue, you know?

Willow and Milestone told the whole
story. They cried when they got to the part
about dropping the statue and breaking it.
They swore that they were always going to
return it, and that they just wanted to teach
Crystal Prep a lesson for playing a prank

on our school. I was sure that Principal Cinch would get angry or yell. But when she heard the statue was broken she just looked really sad. "I was given that statue when I became principal here. It was a gift from the students," she said. "You can't imagine how upsetting this has been."

We all turned to Celestia, waiting for her to give the bag with the statue to Principal Cinch. But instead she just sat there, staring down at it. When she looked up, she was smiling. For a second I thought she was actually **crazy**—why was she smiling about the broken statue?! But then she pulled the statue out of the bag and held it in the air. It was in **one piece again!**

"I know it's not perfect," she said. "But I worked with Ms. Thunderstruck, our science teacher, to repair it. We used a special Bunsen burner to fuse the crystal back together. You really can't tell it was broken, only if you look really, really closely from this one angle."

Principal Cinch leaned in, inspecting the statue. Celestia was right. It looked pretty perfect. Principal Potts, Milestone, and Willow all started smiling, too. "That's amazing," Principal Potts said.

You should have seen the look on Principal Cinch's face! At first she seemed very confused, but then she was just really, really happy. She held the Shadowbolt in her hands and smiled. It sparkled in the light. "It's almost exactly as it was before," she said. "Almost."

It wasn't quite a thank-you, but it was close. I was just relieved we weren't in more trouble....

Luna · 🌙

Dear Diary,

As soon as Principal Cinch saw the statue again, she was a different person. She seemed happier, warmer, and so much kinder than before. I'd spent hours after school repairing the statue with Ms. Thunderstruck, and it was worth it. Cinch even agreed to let us have the Friendship Games again. We're having the Games next Saturday, just three weeks before graduation. It'll be Canterlot High's last big event.

Which is the best news, really. My face hurts from smiling so much. Now we just have to train for the big day. I should really go and tell the team what happened the Games will be here before we know it!

Celestia

Hi, Diary—

This week is going to be **crazy!** We just found out that the Friendship Games will be on Saturday, just a few days away. That means we barely have time to finish making our uniforms, get our team together, and train them so they're prepared for any event. Celestia is finishing class and getting ready to graduate, so she's going to need all the help we can give.

Just this morning I met with Windy Winters and all Celestia's friends. Windy and I are going to finish making the uniforms for our team. Hurricane and two of the girls are going to bake the snacks for the concession stand. Another three kids are painting banners and signs to hang up around the stadium. We're going to have blue-and-gold flags for the Wondercolts, and purple-and-blue flags for the Shadowbolts.

We're making signs for both teams. That way, no matter who you're rooting for, you'll have something to wave in the air.

We tried to get the original Friendship Games team back together, but two of our athletes dropped out. One was too busy with graduation and the other hurt his knee skateboarding. So now I'm practicing archery and rock climbing and the ropes course. I'm trying to get my mile time down because there will probably be a race in the Games. I'm already so nervous thinking about standing there in the middle of the field, hundreds of people watching as I shoot a bow and arrow. I've only been practicing for three hours!

Okay, I better go. There's so much to do, and so little time!

Luna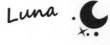

Dear Diary,

Everything is happening so quickly. In just four days we'll have the Friendship Games, and soon I'll be graduating and leaving Canterlot High for good. As each day goes by I get a little sadder, knowing that my time at this school is coming to an end. I'm trying to cherish every moment, but they're going by fast.

Today, I went to the practice for the Friendship Games. As the school president, I'm in charge of welcoming the Shadowbolts and planning the event, so I can't compete on the team.

Thankfully, Windy and Luna have the team running laps and jumping hurdles. Luna had a rock-climbing wall set up in the middle of the field. Each team member had to run toward it, climb over it, then sprint to the goalpost at the end of the field.

Luna went first. **She was great!** She's way faster than most kids, and she climbed the wall easily. But the next two team members had a harder time. Waterfall, a junior with freckles and striped red hair, kept falling. After the fourth time he hit the ground, he gave up and walked off. Then a freshman named Sherbert Burst couldn't get even one foot up the wall. She said the rocks hurt her hands.

I know it's going to be hard to get our team back in shape. It has been months since we had a practice for the Friendship Games, and now there are just a few days to get ready. Windy and Luna told me that everything will come together by Saturday, and I want to believe them. But secretly I'm worried that it's not enough time. They're practicing all afternoon and night the next few days, but will Waterfall really be able to climb the rock wall? Will Luna learn how to shoot a bow and arrow?

I really hope so....

Celestia

Diary...

I'm so tired. **Really, truly tired.** Every muscle in my body hurts.

Today was our last day of practice. We've run miles and miles, scaled rock walls and roller-skated, and shot hundreds of arrows. I even learned how to climb a fifty-foot rope (I was never really good at that before).

Every day for the last four days we've spent hours on the field. Windy taught me how to jump hurdles. Sherbert Burst taught me how to ride a unicycle. I taught Waterfall and Sherbert Burst how to throw a football (because Lavender, one of our teammates, had taught me). Now we just have to hope that all our hard work will pay off.

Principal Potts came to the field after school to visit. We sat down in the grass and she gave us a big pep talk. "You've all worked so hard this week," she said. "You've done your best and that's all I could ever hope for. I want you to know that no matter what happens tomorrow, you've all made me so proud. You're what Canterlot High is all about—perseverance, kindness, and teamwork."

It made me feel better to hear that. There were times this week when I wondered if it was worth it, or if the Crystal Prep team would crush us on Saturday, no matter how hard we tried. Principal Potts reminded me that it isn't about winning or losing. It's about being a part of this special day. The First Annual Friendship Games are happening **tomorrow**, and Celestia and I helped make it happen. I really couldn't ask for anything more.

Luna

Dear Diary,

Today was the First Annual Friendship Games between Crystal Prep and Canterlot High. I hope this day will go down in history. Years from now, after many more Friendship Games have come and gone, people will look back and remember the very first one. This was a big day!

I promised Luna she could write about the end of the Games, so I'll just tell you about the other parts that **I loved**. For me, one of the best moments was walking on the field and seeing everyone in the stands. There were hundreds of people, and so many of them were wearing the Wondercolt colors. My old friend Crescent Moon and I introduced our teams. Night Sky, Luna's friend from middle school, was on the CP team. Luna and Windy had stayed up all night finishing the uniforms, and they were perfect. Everyone on our team wore blue-and-gold bands around their arms, and a humongous blue-and-gold horseshoe on their chests.

It was **amazing** to see how much we had done in so little time. All our friends made snacks for the concession stand. Some sold tickets, others hung up banners and signs. A few kids even acted as ushers, showing people to their seats. Before I knew it, the Games had begun.

When they announced the events, I was so nervous my stomach hurt. But the first event was a relay race, and I knew we had practiced relay races every day for hours, using hurdles and trying to pass the baton off as gracefully as possible. Luna, Hurricane, and Windy were against two girls and a boy from Crystal Prep. They sprinted around the track, jumping hurdles along the way. I'd never actually seen Luna run like that before. She was so fast and graceful. She looked like a real natural!

The Wondercolts won the relay. I was cheering so loudly Principal Potts had to ask me to quiet down (she didn't want Crystal Prep to feel bad). Then there were two more events. Another race, but this time on roller skates. Waterfall, Sherbert Burst, and Lavender were on the Wondercolts team. We tried our best, but the Shadowbolts

123

beat us in the final seconds. Which meant everything came down to the last event— the obstacle course.

I **really** want to tell you what happened, but Luna is sitting right next to me. I told her she could write about the last moments of the Friendship Games. It was more thrilling than I could've ever imagined!

Here she is....

Celestia

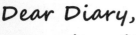

Dear Diary,

I can't wait to tell you about the Friendship Games!!

The obstacle course was the very last event. The score was tied—one to one. Everyone was depending on us to win. All six people on our team had to go through the course. There was a rock wall, a rope to climb, target practice, and then a mad sprint to the end. I wasn't sure how we were going to do. The rock wall had been such a problem for us before!

We were in the lead at first. Windy and I went through pretty fast, but I had some trouble getting a bull's-eye with my bow and arrow. Then Waterfall and Autumn Frost went.

Autumn Frost had a really hard time with the rock wall, and Waterfall almost gave up when he couldn't get a bull's-eye after the first five tries. Little by little, the Shadowbolts caught up to us. Then they were in the lead for a bit.

Lavender was the last person to go on our team. She went through as fast as she could, and was able to catch up to the Crystal Prep girl who was shooting at her target. Lavender got a bull's-eye on the first try! But then, as she was running toward the finish line, she tripped. The Shadowbolt ran past her. Lavender got up and sprinted to catch her, but they finished right at the same time. It was a tie!! After all that,

<u>A TIE!!!</u>

Principal Potts and Principal Cinch were standing beside the giant gold trophy. Everyone looked confused. What were we supposed to do now? Who had won? Who would get the trophy? Would there be a tiebreaker or something?

Before anyone could say anything, Celestia stepped forward. She picked up the trophy, holding it high in the air. "It seems like we have a tie," she said. The people in the stands were shouting. They didn't seem happy, but she went on. "I want to give this trophy to the Shadowbolts as a sign of our friendship. So much has happened this year, and it means a lot that we are all here today, celebrating. Here's to reuniting friends, new and old! May there be many more Friendship Games!"

At first I was upset. I kept thinking, **Celestia! No!! What are you doing?! We can't let them win!!** But then I saw the look on the other team's faces. They were so shocked that we would just give them the trophy. That we wouldn't make them compete with us to decide who deserved to win. In that moment, we really were friends.

It seemed like everyone in the stands agreed, too, because they broke out in cheers. First everyone sang the Wondercolt fight song, then everyone sang a song for the Shadowbolts. After that, Celestia gave a speech, thanking me and Windy for all our help this week. I've never been so proud to be her sister. She said she couldn't have done it without us. Yes, we bicker sometimes, and sometimes it annoys me that Celestia is such a perfectionist, but Canterlot High isn't going to be the same without her. What am I going to do without her around next year?

Luna

Dear Diary,

This morning I opened up the <u>Canterlot Gazette</u>. **Finally**, there was a story that didn't make my stomach hurt.

The headline read:

Canterlot High Gives Crystal Prep Trophy as a Sign of Friendship

It told the whole story of the Games, and how there had been a tie at the end. It said we were such kind and generous hosts. It said that we showed such good sportsmanship. It even had a picture of me handing the trophy to Crescent Moon. She looked stunned. (I kind of wished they showed the moment after, when we hugged and Crescent Moon told me how much she had missed me.)

It seems like everyone is talking about the Games now. Just today, Luna overheard people in the park saying how impressed they were with Canterlot High. "Then she just gave them the trophy!" one woman said. "No one could believe it! How generous is that? Whatever happened before, that's obviously not the full story. How did that rumor get started?!"

The best part is, the two Crystal Prep boys who'd painted our Wondercolt came forward and confessed. They said they just felt too guilty, especially after we gave the trophy to Crystal Prep. Principal Potts decided that she wouldn't ask that they be punished if they volunteered this weekend. They're going to help us break down all the equipment from the Friendship Games, clean up the bleachers, and make sure Canterlot High looks exactly like it did before hundreds of people poured into our stadium. I have to admit, it felt good to see Principal Cinch's face when the boys confessed. She accompanied them to Principal Potts's office and apologized for saying her students had nothing to do with it. Turns out we were right after all.

Principal Cinch has put the crystal Shadowbolt back on its pedestal in the main hall, where everyone can see it (if you look very closely, you might notice the tiny crack). I've heard from some people that she's smiling a bit more than usual. I think things might actually be back to normal or close to it. Luna asked Principal Potts about next year's Games, but she said they might change it to once every four years, to make it really special. I guess we'll see. Now all I have to worry about is finishing up classes, and my speech for graduation.

I've already started writing it. It makes me sad thinking of saying good-bye to everyone, so I'm not going to. Instead I'm going to say "see you soon," because just like our friends who went to Crystal Prep, I know our paths will cross again. At college. Or after college. Or maybe after that.

I hope that wherever I go, and whatever I do, I'll be able to come back to Canterlot High someday. Maybe I could be a teacher or a coach. Maybe I could work in the science department, like Ms. Thunderstruck. Maybe I could even be principal.

That probably sounds crazy. **But a girl can dream, can't she?**

Celestia